Snippy the Crab Caught on Camera

Alison Miles

ISBN: 978-1-915130-01-3

For Alastair whose beautiful voice
soothes my soul and warms my heart.

Welcome Sir Davy to Cocklebed Bay
DB 001
POLICE
COCKLEBED HARBOUR 'TUBBY'

EXCITEMENT rebounded round Cocklebed Bay
That blowy and blustery October day.
A special event was about to occur:
A film crew was gathered causing a stir.

The old harbour walls were crowded with people.
The church bell tolled ten in the granite grey steeple.
Natter and chatter babbled about.
What a glorious thing – the whole town turned out!

Up rolled a car, sleek, shiny and black,
PC Panton was ready to keep the crowd back.
Out climbed a gentleman, distinguished and tall,
"Sir Davy Battenburger!" a girl **GASPED** in thrall!

Half up the steps ready and waiting,
Snippy and cousin were hotly debating.
Could they get near the action they both longed to see: —
The great man and his Triton tear out to sea?

"Follow me," **CHUCKLED** Freda. "I know just the place."
And the two little crabs raced along at a pace.
They dodged between wellies and pushchairs and prams,
Twixt grandmas and grandpas and even two lambs!
"Over there," pointed Freda, and scrammed up a ladder.
Snippy struggled to follow – it was quite a palaver!

Fragile
Nikon

The camera crew bustled the length of the pier,
Backwards and forwards lugging their gear.
For their voyage was **DEEPER** than ever before,
Exploring new regions – a treat was in store!

Snippy and Freda perched snug in a life ring,
Hearts beating hard with excitement near stifling,
For right underneath them, with just room for a few,
Was the cool submarine with its 360 view.

Sir Davy was helped off the old wooden jetty
By the clever producer whose first name was Betty.
Snippy, delighted, craned out to see more
But the silky-smooth ring slipped under his claw...
AAHHHHHHHHHHH! Off he slithered, slicing the air,
While Freda looked on with a horrified stare.
He skimmed past Sir Davy just missing his ear
And straight after that he whizzed past the pier!

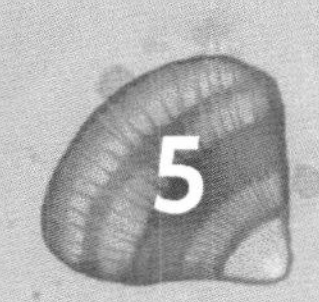

SLAP-SPLAAAASSHHH!

In he plunged spiralling down,
Like a whirligig beetle spinning around.
"Humph!" he thought huffily, calming his nerves,
"This surely is NOT what a shore crab deserves!"

Then **ROOOAAAARRRR...** went the engines and turmoil began:
The water frothed up like a great boiling pan.
Snippy was tossed about this way and that,
Till **SPLAT!** He was caught like a car windscreen gnat!

The sub started moving. The crowd wildly cheered
And thrusting fast forward the craft disappeared.
Onwards it **SPED** to the ocean's far reaches,
A dare-daunting distance from any known beaches.

Search beams fanned ahead lighting their way
With Snippy stuck fast in doleful dismay.
A crack gaped below gashing open the bed,
A zigzagging scar of deep ocean dread...
"YIKES!" simpered Snippy. "That's no place to dwell."
And he frizzled a shiver all over his shell.

The Triton bore onwards, closer and closer
Relentlessly forwards, a baleful bulldozer...
AHHHHHHHHH...
ARRRRRRGGGHH! In they slipped,
  beneath the earth's crust;
Snippy's shell crushed with pressure ready to bust.
Blackness entombed them, catacomb cold;
Snippy's tummy turned over with dread unforetold...
But the cave, he observed, shone a myriad lights
And he swivelled his eyes to a world of delights:

Strange animals flip-flapped and slithered and swam.
Sir Davy expounded a great dithyramb.
His master narration kept building the tension
As all round the globe people gawped in suspension...
"And now, the first view of this pristine new world..."
His velvet-voiced monologue richly unfurled...

From China to Iceland, and Chad to Peru
Folks goggled their screens in a worldwide to-do...

The sub hovered steady...
The cameraman ready...
"Switch view!" Betty ordered, tapping the dashboard.
Sir Davy's kind face beamed calm and assured.
The world held its breath. But what did it see...?
Snippy's **CHEEKY** wee face caught on camera three!

Children from everyplace shrieked with delight;
Their cheery bright faces the happiest sight.
But Betty was fretty. This just wouldn't do:
In a serious programme? What a taboo!

"**QUICK!** Roll the sub," Betty yelled at the captain,
Whose mind was well-trained and his reflex
fast-acting.
The Triton turned over; its bottom on top
And away from the lens Snippy pinged with a **POP!**
Sprawling he tumbled all head over heels,
Adrift 'mongst the blob fish and candescent eels.

Columns of gases, red, green and blue,
Rose in great clouds from a magical brew,
Giving off vapours horribly hot –
Would he be boiled alive in this witch's stew pot?

His legs wouldn't move and he started to sink,
Descending on down through the gluey-goo ink,
Plumbing the depths of this ocean ravine —
A place where a shore crab should never be seen!

He sploshed on the floor of this undersea cave.
Abandoned by all, his future looked grave.
Lost deep **UNDERGROUND** in this devilish place
What creatures were these? – not one friendly face:

Viperfish! Fangtooths! Two terrible beasts,
Who gulp down their dinner in feverish feasts.
And dragonfish, **GHOULISH** and **GHASTLY** to see,
Hunting their luncheon in ravaging spree.

The nautilus, deep in this world without light,
Crunches on crabs to grab a light bite.
And oldest of all the great coelacanth,
Who swam with the dinosaurs long before man,
Darts through the caverns scouring for squid
As his ancestors for seamless millennia did!

A rumbling started, grinding and gnawing;
The sound of a giant's chest thund'rously snoring.
The ground began quaking,
Snippy's legs shilly-shaking...

BAAAAALLOOOSHHHH! Through the floor burst an undersea geyser
With the titanic force of a mega-blast freezer.
Snippy shot sharply upwards at rocket-fuelled pace,
Straight for the crack – would there be enough space?

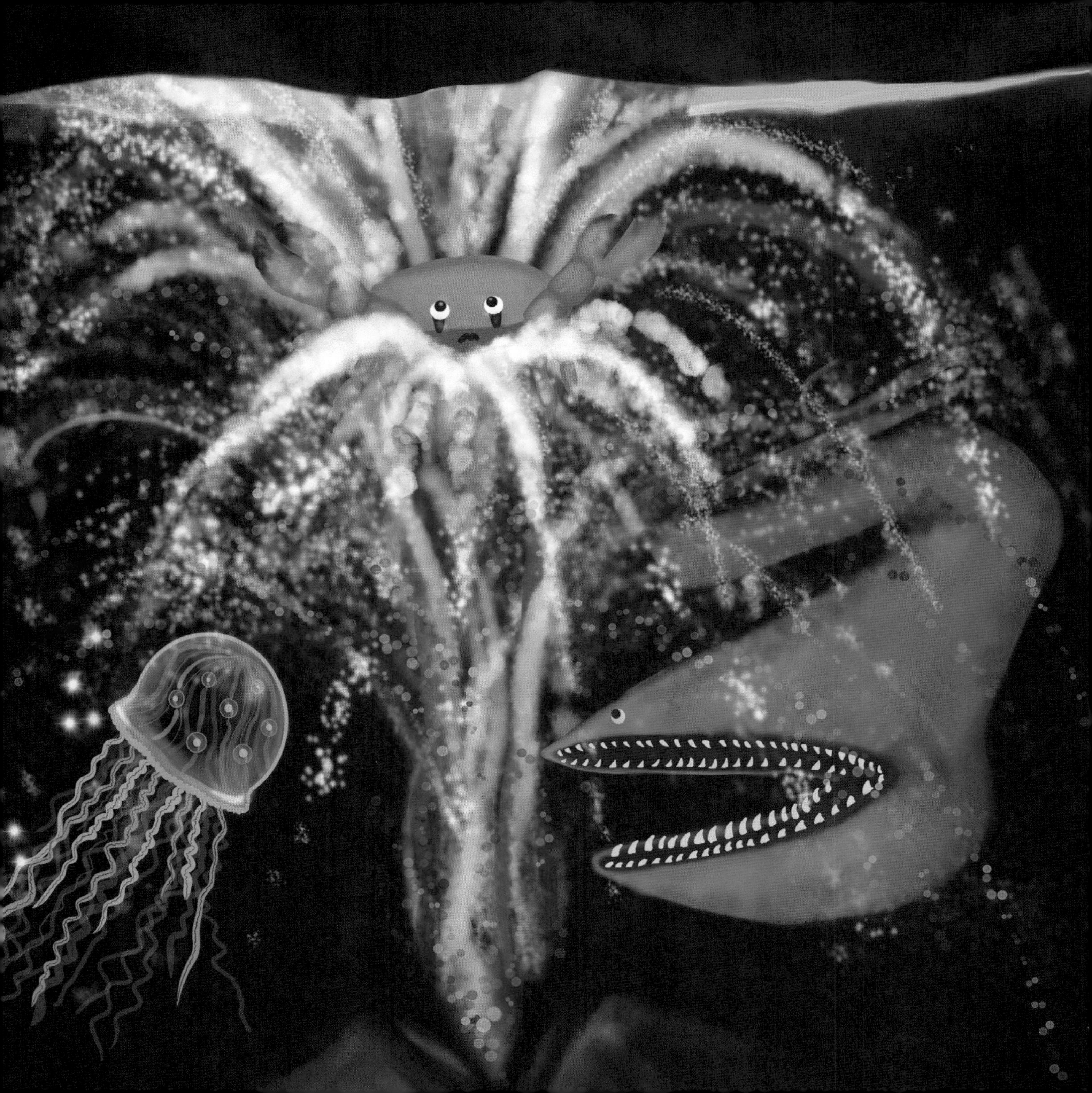

But **TONK!** he got jammed in the jaw-jagged crack,
Torrents rushed up past his front and his back.
He wiggled his legs with all of his might.
He jiggled and strained and put up a fight,
But the harder he struggled, the **TIGHTER** he stuck.
Would his life be spent here? What crabawful luck!

Exhausted, he slumped with a snippisome sigh
And a few **TINY** tears brimmed up in his eye.
He was oodlesome lonely and scrutiously scared.
"I know what I'll do. I'll sing!" he declared.
So he opened his mouth and deep from his chest
His crabbisome voice rang out with great zest!

He warbled some Mozart, some Verdi and Brahms.
EXTRAVAGANT gestures flailed with his arms
While the sumptuous music filled up his soul
And made him forget he was stuck in a hole.

But down out of sight, a predator lurked.
He had heard Snippy's song and was igglesome irked.
For Otto was sleepy and having a nap
And he did NOT like opera, this eight-legged chap.
But when he saw Snippy, small, juicy and **PLUMP**,
His eyes glowed with glee and his heart gave a thump.
He lumbered on out of his deep hidden dwelling
And crept towards Snippy, his appetite swelling.
Yet just as his tentacles reached for his prey
(With Snippy still lost in bel canto display!...)

BOOOFFFF! came a thwack which threw him aside—
A huge purple beanbag sent for a ride.
Snippy's eyes were on stalks; he had not the least
hunch
That he'd nearly been crunched up as octopus lunch!

Sand **SWIRLED** around in an undersea storm;
Could Snippy make out a blurry grey form?
"Is it Megan?" he thought. "No, I surely am
dreaming..."
But he peeked through his claws and there, broadly
beaming,
Were Megan and Merlin from Cocklebed Bay.
They had tracked the slick Triton this far-distant way
And raced to this treacherous, outlandish spot
To rescue their crab friend, no matter what!

So they dug in their noses to give him a nudge.
They prised with their flippers; he just wouldn't budge.
Then Merlin, who loved Mrs Wong's old string bag,
And never let go of that soggy old rag,
Had an idea – and a fine one indeed!
He wasted no time, acting at speed
And placing the handles in Snippy's wee pincers,
He clamped them both shut – they were capable mincers!
Then he turned on his tail and tore fast away;
Snippy's arms were pulled taught (to his pain and dismay!)
Like two rubber bands ready to snap,
Stretching longer and longer, the poor little chap...

POP! FFFFSHWEEEEE!

Out he shot like a cork from a bottle,
Careening along like a car at full throttle.
The salt stung his eyes and he screwed up his face
As they raced towards home at a shell-splitting pace.

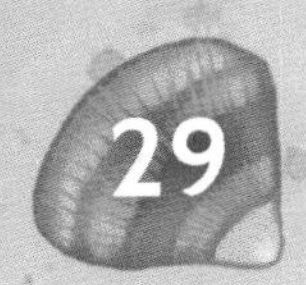

When at last they were far from that terrible spot
And the scaverous cavern a dim distant dot,
Snippy's arms were worn out and he started to flag,
So Megan popped Snippy in Merlin's mesh bag.
He slumped to the bottom **EXHAUSTED** but happy.
What wonderful friends, he was one lucky chappy!
Then Megan and Merlin took off through the tide
Leaping the waves in one rollicking ride!

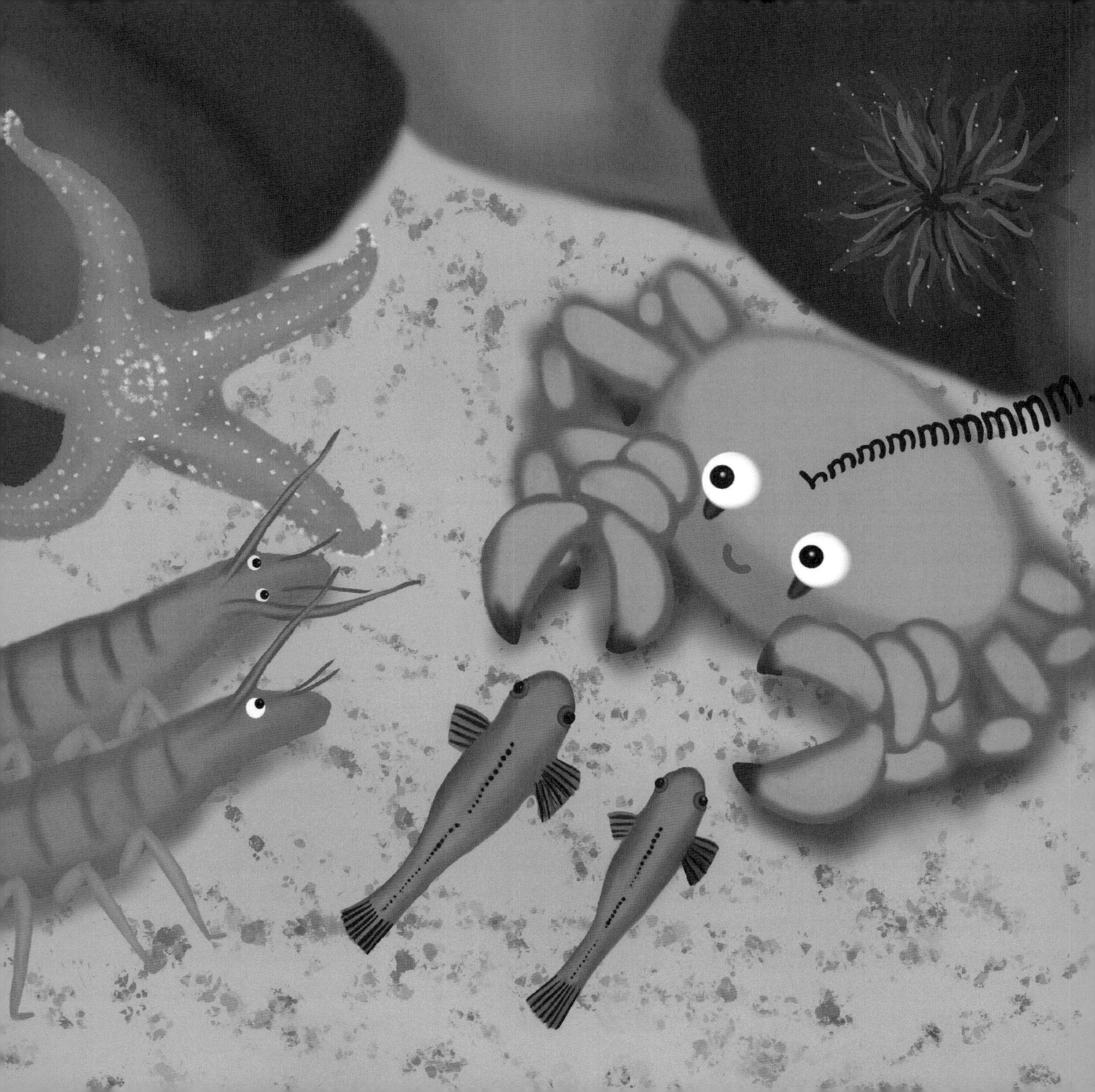
hmmmmmmmm.

Let us mention no more of that **TERRIBLE** day;
Snippy made it back home – that is all we should say.
He wobbled his way straight into his lair
And snuggled right down like a wintering bear.

He saw out the autumn and chill winter, too,
Without leaving his home – well, that wouldn't do!
"Have you done with **EXPLORING?**"
His friends asked imploring.
But Snippy just smiled and sat perfectly still,
Humming himself a Rossini Quadrille!
His friends had grown used to the triumphs and terrors
Of Snippy's swashbucklingly vagabond errors.
And they heaved a great sigh, for they'd all have to wait,
To find out for sure what might be Snippy's fate...

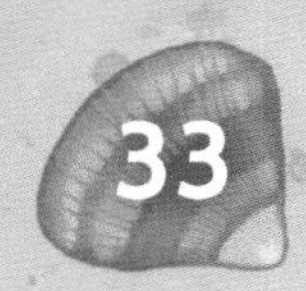

Printed in Poland
by Amazon Fulfillment
Poland Sp. z o.o., Wrocław